BEYOND THE MOUNTAINS

COMING TO AMERICA FROM HAITI—1991

KATHLEEN M. MULDOON

Perfection Learning®

Design: Tobi Cunningham
Illustration: Greg Hargreaves

Cover Image Credit: Digital Stock

Dèyè mòn gen mòn.
Beyond the mountains, there are more
mountains.
—Creole Proverb

Dedication
To Rick Yurcheshen—a colleague, confidant,
and friend

Acknowledgement
Many thanks to Dimy Doresca for his
thoughtful review of this story.

For information, contact
Perfection Learning® Corporation
1000 North Second Avenue, P.O. Box 500
Logan, Iowa 51546-0500.
Phone: 1-800-831-4190 • Fax: 1-800-543-2745
perfectionlearning.com

Paperback ISBN 0-7891-5853-1
Cover Craft® ISBN 0-7569-0974-1

TABLE OF CONTENTS

INTRODUCTION

HAITI IN 1991

For the people of Haiti, 1991 started as a wonderful year. That is when Jean-Bertrand Aristide became president.

People had voted for him at the end of 1990. It was the first time ever that Haitians had free elections. This time, soldiers could not keep the people from voting.

Haitians expected great things from their new president. They were tired of cruel leaders. **Dictators** and soldiers had ruled Haiti ever since it gained **independence** from France in 1804.

Most Haitians were poor farmers. They could barely grow enough to feed their own families. The harsh leaders of the past had kept the country's riches for themselves.

People who spoke against the cruel leaders were beaten and killed. By 1990, Haitian people were angry. They came together and forced the government to let them vote.

President Aristide tried to be a fair leader. He invited poor people to the National Palace. He served them meals.

Aristide wanted to give farmers more land. He wanted to raise poor people's pay. He announced that he was firing the top army officers.

The soldiers were angry. They were used to getting anything they wanted from the president.

So in September 1991, General Raoul Cedras took over the government. He and his soldiers moved into the palace. President Aristide escaped to Venezuela. He later went to the United States.

General Cedras was as cruel as other leaders. His soldiers hunted and killed the people who had helped elect Aristide.

The year was not turning out as the people had hoped. Some people hid in the mountains of Haiti. Others fled in small boats. They tried to reach safer countries, such as Cuba and the United States.

The people of Haiti had many problems. But they never lost their spirit and hope.

THE UNITED STATES IN 1991

United States soldiers were also busy in 1991. Many fought in the Persian Gulf War in January and February.

George Bush was president. He worked to keep drugs from coming into the country. He also promised Americans that he would not raise taxes.

But the government spent more money than it raised. Finally Congress had to raise taxes to pay the country's bills. This made people angry. In 1992 they would elect William Clinton president.

The United States stopped giving money to Haiti in October 1991. This is because once again Haitian soldiers had taken control of their country.

Many Haitian refugees tried to come to the United States. The U.S. Coast Guard watched for their boats. They took the **refugees** to a U.S. Navy base in Cuba.

Haitian refugees had to prove that their lives were in danger in Haiti. Those who could were allowed to enter the United States. Many went to live in Miami, Florida. A large community of Haitian **immigrants** already lived there. Those who could not prove their lives were in danger were returned to Haiti.

Americans enjoyed new types of entertainment in 1991. Television and radio talk shows were popular. More families bought personal computers.

Alternative music became more popular. The first alternative rock festival called Lollapalooza was held.

In 1991, people began planning for the new **millennium**. It was just nine years away.

COMING TO AMERICA FROM HAITI
1991

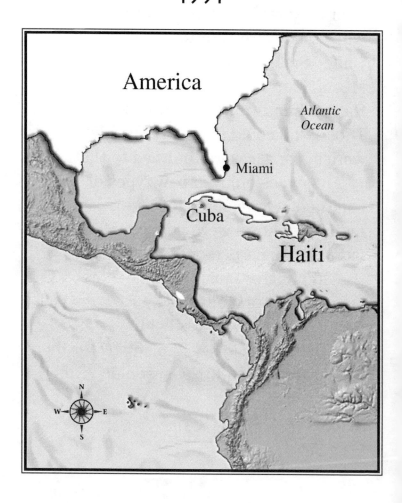

1

WHERE'S PAPI?

September 29, 1991
    This morning **Manmi**, Michele, and
I were weeding our sweet potato
patch. Everything seemed normal.

Suddenly, we heard loud noises. We looked down the mountain toward the sounds.

"Gunshots!" Manmi cried.

"And smoke!" Michele added.

Manmi and I looked at each other. **Papi** had told us that soldiers might attack the president's palace.

He worried that they might hurt or kill President Aristide. Nine months ago, Papi and other **Lavalas** followers helped elect Aristide. I had helped too.

I looked back down the mountain. I could barely see the National Palace through the smoke. Was our president alive?

I could not eat dinner. Sounds of gunfire still floated up the mountain. For once, Michele kept quiet. Manmi looked scared.

They are asleep now. I am too worried to sleep. The worst thing of all is that Papi has not come home.

October 4, 1991

For days, I have tried to stay strong for Manmi and Michele. At 13, I should be a man. But my insides feel like mush.

Word has spread up the mountain. President Aristide escaped. But soldiers are hunting down and killing those who supported him. I pray that Papi is in hiding.

I keep busy doing Papi's chores and mine. This morning, Manmi sent Michele to help me haul water.

"Is Papi alive?" she asked.

"Of course," I said.

I do feel in my heart that he is alive.

We carried our buckets toward the house. Suddenly I stopped. Soldiers stood in the doorway. I dropped the water and ran toward them.

Manmi stood outside. Tears ran down her face.

"He is not here!" she shouted.

I stood beside her and looked through the open door. The soldiers had torn up our one-room home.

One came outside. He grabbed my shirt.

"Who are you?" he demanded.

"Louis Dupree," I said.

"Are you Henri Dupree's son?" he asked.

I nodded. He pulled me toward him and shook me. He stuck his face in mine.

"We will find him," he snarled.

Finally, he and the others headed up the mountain to the next village. They took Papi's rifle with them.

Now I am the only protection Manmi and Michele have.

2

WHAT MAMBO AMIE SAID

October 10, 1991

The soldiers have been back almost every day. Yesterday, they burned our potato patch. They were angry because they could not find Papi.

They didn't know that Manmi and I had picked almost all the potatoes. We dug a hole and hid them in the ground.

Today, we dug some up for Manmi and Michele to sell at the market.

Manmi made Michele dress in my old clothes. She wants the soldiers to think Michele is a boy.

"That's because I'm pretty," Michele said. She tossed her head. "They might want me for a girlfriend."

I laughed to myself. Who would want skinny Michele for a girlfriend?

I helped Manmi load two baskets of potatoes. Michele and Manmi put the baskets on their heads. Then they started down the mountain trail. The market is in the next village.

I watched until they were out of sight. Then I prepared for my own trip. I had planned it last night when I could not sleep.

I had first thought about taking Manmi and Michele to join some neighbors. They had escaped up the mountain. They were hiding in caves, waiting for the soldiers to get tired of hunting them. But how would Papi find us?

By sunup, I had decided to visit **Mambo** Amie after Manmi left for the market. Didn't Papi always visit her when he needed advice?

Before leaving I found my **vaccine**. I hadn't played it since the soldiers came. But I knew Mambo Amie would want me to play.

Mambo Amie was the smartest woman in the village. Her **hounfor** was at the edge of the village.

On the way there, I kept looking over my shoulder. The soldiers were nowhere in sight.

Mambo Amie met me at the door. She hugged me and pulled me inside.

"I've been waiting for you," she said. "I hear your papi is gone."

I nodded. I tried not to cry.

"I need to know if we should hide or not," I said. "Should we go up the mountain?"

Mambo Amie did not answer. Instead, she lit many candles. She motioned for me to play my vaccine.

After I blew the first few notes, Mambo Amie beat her drum. She banged it slowly at first. Then she played faster and faster! I swayed and moved to the music. I felt Mambo Amie's energy pour into me.

Finally, we both stopped. I sank to the ground. Mambo Amie closed her eyes. Everything grew very quiet.

"Your papi will come," she said at last. "Go home and wait for him."

I played a merry tune on the way home. I didn't care if the soldiers heard or not.

Even Michele and Manmi were smiling when they came home. They had sold all the potatoes. Manmi buried the coins they had earned.

I didn't tell Manmi and Michele what Mambo Amie said. But we all seemed to sense that something good was about to happen.

I know I will sleep tonight.

3

PAPI'S PLAN

October 11, 1991

I dreamed that the soldiers were chasing me. I had almost made it home when one grabbed my shoulder.

"Stop!" I started to yell. A hand covered my mouth.

I opened my eyes. I was on my bed. It was dark. But someone's hand still covered my mouth.

"It's me," a voice whispered in the darkness.

Papi? I pulled his hand from my mouth and threw my arms around him.

"Shh," he warned. By now, Manmi and Michele were awake.

Papi moved into the middle of the room where moonlight shone. He wore a dress and a wig! I laughed until I cried.

"I'm sorry, Papi," I said when I could catch my breath. "But you make one ugly woman!"

Papi laughed too. "I know, Louis. But there is a reason for it. My time is short. Gather around and listen carefully."

We huddled around Papi. I didn't want to let him go.

"It is no longer safe here," Papi said. "Tomorrow night, we will sail for freedom.

We will go to America."

"Hurrah!" shouted Michele.

"Hush," Manmi said. "Please, Michele, you must be quiet and listen."

Papi nodded. "None of you must say a word to anyone. Tomorrow night, the clouds will cover the moon. After dark, you climb down the dark side of the mountain. You will meet me by the rocky cove."

"What shall we bring?" Manmi asked.

"Nothing!" Papi said. "There will be no room on the boat for anything but you."

Papi hugged us all. Then as quick as a wink, he was gone.

All day, we tried to pretend things were normal. I told my friend Tony I'd see him tomorrow. But I knew that was not true.

October 13, 1991

I am writing this on a rocking boat. All I have left of Haiti is this notebook, my vaccine, and the clothes I am wearing.

Late last night, we followed Papi's plan. Michele, Manmi, and I put on dark clothes. Clouds covered the moon.

As we started down the mountain, I looked back toward our little house.

"I'll be back someday," I promised it.

Halfway down the mountain, we heard the soldiers coming toward us. Michele started crying. I grabbed her and Manmi and pulled them into a shrub.

"Don't move!" I warned. "Be as still as statues."

The soldiers passed by. They sang and cursed loudly. They were drunk.

Soon we continued our journey to the cove. Papi waited there. This **rickety** boat, in which I now sit, waited. About 40 other people were already packed into it.

As soon as we boarded, the boat pulled out into the water. We sailed away from Haiti and toward America.

A part of me feels happy. I want to take out my vaccine and play freedom songs.

But we are not free yet.

4

ON THE SEA

October 14, 1991

I played my vaccine for the first time today. The few kids who were not seasick enjoyed it. For a little while, they sang.

Manmi and Michele threw up yesterday and this morning. By afternoon, the boat rocked less.

"I think we have smooth sailing ahead," Papi said.

That's what I love about Papi. When things look the darkest, he finds something to smile about.

I made a new friend. Nicolas is 12. The soldiers in Haiti killed his father. Now he and his **granme** are going to America. She is very old and weak.

Papi divided a loaf of bread among those who could eat. Later, he and I stood by the boat rail. Choppy, green water surrounded the boat as far as we could see.

"When will we reach America?" I asked.

Papi put his hand on my shoulder. "Two days, maybe three. Jean Paul is a good sailor. He will do his best."

We are sailing in Jean Paul's fishing boat. People pack every inch. The small cabin is not large enough for more than a few people to squeeze into. Most of us sleep on the deck. Michele and I use Manmi's lap for a pillow.

Michele is over being seasick. Manmi is too. But sometimes she coughs and cannot stop. Papi says that might be from the cold sea air.

The sea is bumpy again. I hope we'll awake to a calm day.

October 16, 1991

Last night, Nicolas's granme died. There was no way to bury her. Papi helped Jean Paul lower her body into the ocean.

Nicolas cried and cried. So did everyone else. Papi said a prayer while I played a soft song on my vaccine.

Papi and Manmi promised to take care of Nicolas when we reach America. I'll have my very own brother!

Two of the men caught enough fish for everyone to eat. Most of the people who had been seasick seem to be better.

I was just beginning to believe we really might reach America safely. Then I heard something I was not meant to hear.

Tonight Jean Paul left the sailing to his first mate. He came out of the cabin and found Papi.

"We have trouble," he whispered. "There is nothing ahead but rough water. We are sailing into a storm."

"We can't turn back," Papi replied. "If we do, we will be killed."

Jean Paul nodded. "Better to die here than there."

I felt my body turn to stone. Giant goose bumps popped up on my skin. Inside, I felt as cold and slimy as the fish I had eaten.

Now I don't want to put away my notebook. I am afraid I will never be able to write in it again.

5

STORM!

October 17, 1991

I hope that someday I will be able to read this. Each time the boat hits a wave, my writing goes off the page.

Now the boat is bouncing on the waves. People are holding onto whatever they can. Nicolas is holding onto Manmi. Michele's arms are wrapped around Papi.

I am crammed between everyone. I could not move if I wanted to!

The storm hit before the sun came up. The wind tossed saltwater sprays in my face. No one could walk without slipping on the wet deck.

"I'm scared, Papi!" wailed Michele when the water first hit her.

Other children on the boat cried too. Manmi and the other adults looked frightened.

"You boys look after the folks out here," Papi said to Nicolas and me. "I'm going to the cabin to help Jean Paul."

I tried to play some music, but the wind blew water into my flute. Nicolas started telling a story to the children. They were too scared to listen.

Soon we gave up and just sat with

Michele and Manmi. The wind whipped around and through us. It seemed to shake the whole world.

This afternoon, a giant wave washed over the **stern** of the boat. It knocked a man and a girl overboard. It happened so fast that no one could save them.

Right now I wish I were back in Haiti. I am hungry and thirsty. There is water all around us. But it is loaded with salt, and we cannot drink it.

Papi just came back. His face looks grim. He says that the worst of the storm is coming. He sits and puts his long arms around Manmi and Michele. He calls for Nicolas and me to come closer.

I have to stop writing now and hold on. I wonder what it feels like to drown.

6

RESCUED

October 18, 1991

    I am no longer on Jean Paul's boat.
Since I wrote yesterday, our plans and
lives have changed forever.

The storm hit with the force of a thousand soldiers. The wind threw us about like dead leaves.

Papi made us hold on to the rail. Tied below was a rubber raft. Papi grabbed the end of the rope.

"If we go down, swim for the raft," he yelled.

I didn't know if anyone else heard him. The wind blew his words out to sea.

Suddenly, the boat heaved. It seemed to break in half. Before I knew what was happening, I was bobbing in the ocean. Below the darkening sky, I saw Jean Paul's boat upside down in the water.

"Here, Louis!" Papi shouted. I could barely make him out as he hauled people into the yellow raft.

I swam like I never swam before. My arms ached. The weight of my clothes pulled me down. But just when I thought I would drown, strong arms hauled me into the raft.

Manmi and Michele laughed and cried at the same time when they saw me.

"Where's Nicolas?" I asked when I could talk again.

"Here I am!"

Nicolas threw his arms around me. He looked like a drowned rat. We held each other tight.

Papi had pulled 16 people into the raft. It drifted farther from the **capsized** boat.

Between the wind gusts, we heard people calling for help. We could not see them. Even if we could, we had no way to reach them. The oars on the raft were no match for the swirling water.

As we watched in horror, Jean Paul's boat sank from sight.

"Good-bye, Jean Paul," Papi whispered. A tear rolled down his face.

Michele, Manmi, Nicolas, and I stared at the sea. I thought about the other 20 people that had not made it to the raft.

Just as the storm grew quiet, a ship whistle blasted nearby.

"The United States Coast Guard!" said one of the men on the raft.

An enormous ship pulled up beside us. Before I knew it, the Coast Guard had hauled each of us onto their ship. They gave us blankets.

As I wrapped mine around me, I was surprised to see my notebook and pencil peeking out of my wet pocket. But my vaccine must have fallen into the water.

Members of the Coast Guard do not speak **Creole** like we do. They seem nice, though.

Most of the rescued people are sleeping. But I can't. I keep thinking about what Papi learned a little while ago.

We all thought that the Coast Guard ship was taking us to America. But Papi talked with the captain. Papi speaks English, French, and Creole!

After his meeting, Papi slipped his arm around Manmi and me.

"We are not going to the United States just yet," he said. "We are going to Cuba."

"Cuba! But why, Papi?" I asked.

"They have a camp there," he explained. "We must go there first—with other people who have fled Haiti. We must prove our lives will be in danger if they send us back to Haiti. If we do, then they will let us go to the United States."

"Oh, Henri," Manmi said. "They must let us! If we go back, we will be killed."

Papi pulled her to him.

"It's out of our hands," he said. "Right now, just be glad we are alive."

I am trying to do what Papi says. I am trying to be glad that we survived. I'm also glad I have a new brother.

But I am not glad that we're being taken to Cuba. I want to be free! Now!

7

THE CAMP

October 25, 1991

I can't believe we have been at this camp for a week. It's very boring.

The Coast Guard brought us here to Guantanomo Bay. It is in Cuba. We are being held at an old Navy base. The men running it call it "Gitmo."

My family and Nicolas share a tent with several other families. It's a dull green color. The floor is tar. Papi said it used to be an airplane runway.

Every day, the Coast Guard ships bring more people to Gitmo. All have fled from Haiti.

The day after we arrived, Navy men and immigration officials talked to us. We were afraid that they would make Nicolas go to a tent at the other end of the camp. That is where they keep the **orphan** children.

But Papi convinced them that Nicolas was his son. Papi always taught me not to lie. But I understand why he lied this time.

"I'm bored," Michele whined yesterday. "When can we go to America? When can we leave?"

"You must be patient," Manmi sighed.

She looks very tired. Her cough is worse. Sometimes she coughs most of the night.

"The food is awful," Michele continued. "It tastes like cardboard."

Manmi didn't answer. I frowned at Michele. But inside, I felt the same way that she did.

October 28, 1991

This morning, Papi talked to the immigration people. They told him that it would be a few weeks before our hearing. That is when they will tell us if we can go to America.

Papi brought us something exciting! It was a letter from **Tant** Gisele and **Monnonk** Claude.

Papi's sister and her husband had fled to America in 1981. I was only 3 years old. I do not remember them. But they never forget my birthday!

Papi read the letter.

My dear brother,
  Claude and I wait for the day
that you can come to Miami. We
have two rooms ready for you in our
home. Henri, we can find you work
right away. You will be in your own
place in no time.

  Love,
  Gisele

Papi smiled.

"Now I can tell the officials that we have a place to live in America," he said. "I can tell them that I will have a job too."

This afternoon, some doctors examined our family. I didn't understand their English. But I knew when they said "OK" because that has the same meaning in Creole.

"OK," the doctor said after looking in my eyes and throat.

He said "OK" after looking at Papi, Michele, and Nicolas. But he frowned after listening to Manmi's chest. He checked her all over. Then he sent her to another part of the medical tent.

Papi talked to the doctor in English.

"They are just going to take a picture of her chest," Papi told us. "The doctor is worried because Manmi coughs a lot. He also wants to know what is making her so tired all the time. She will be right back."

But Manmi did not come back. The doctor told Papi that Manmi has a disease called **tuberculosis**. They took her away and said we cannot see her for a while.

"She will be OK," Papi told us. He tried to smile.

Nicolas and I are running out of ways to entertain Michele. Nicolas is a great storyteller. I make up good games.

But without Manmi, nothing matters. I worry that they will send her back to Haiti. I worry more that she will die.

8

ENSIGN JONES

November 13, 1991

Every day that passes seems a hundred hours long. Each one is exactly like the one before. The only change now is that we can visit Manmi.

She is getting better slowly. The doctors gave her some new medicine. They let us visit her a little each day.

"Soon I will be back in the tent telling you all what to do," Manmi said this morning. "You all better be sure it's clean and swept."

Michele frowned.

"You know I've been doing everything," she said.

Nicolas and I looked at each other and burst out laughing.

"Yes, Manmi," I said. "She does all the moaning and complaining."

Manmi laughed. She was able to laugh without coughing!

"It will be good to hear her again," Manmi said.

November 14, 1991

This afternoon a new person came to Gitmo. He told us his name is Cletus Jones. He is an **ensign**.

He is the first to even tell us his name. The exciting thing is that he speaks some Creole!

"My mother is Haitian," he explained.

Ensign Jones came to see us after supper. He even brought each of us some candy. He was dressed in jeans instead of his uniform.

"Do you play basketball?" he asked.

"Sort of," Nicolas said. "At home, I had nailed up an old fruit basket. I practiced with a soccer ball."

"Louis plays," Michele bragged before I could open my mouth. "He played down in the village with a real basketball!"

Ensign Jones grinned. "I'll see you after work tomorrow. I'll have a surprise for you."

I think things are going to be a lot better with Ensign Jones around.

November 16, 1991

Yesterday, Ensign Jones and three other sailors put up a basketball hoop on a pole near our tent. One man brought a real basketball.

Michele, Nicolas, and I started playing with them right away. Soon some other kids from the tent joined us.

The time passed quickly! Then right before dark, Ensign Jones took out a harmonica. He played some lively tunes. How I wished I had my vaccine to play with him!

This afternoon, even Papi joined the game. When we all became tired, Ensign Jones came and sat inside our tent.

"Manmi's coming back tomorrow," Michele told him.

Ensign Jones grinned.

"I know. And I know something else too. Your hearing is coming up soon. Maybe you'll be in Miami with your aunt and uncle by Thanksgiving!"

He explained the American holiday.

"I have been told that these hearings are hard," Papi said.

"Yes, sir," Ensign Jones admitted. "You must convince the officials that you are in danger if you return to Haiti. That is the only way you will be allowed to go to America."

"But of course we would be killed!" Papi said. "What do they think would happen?"

"You and I know that, sir," Ensign Jones said. "But you must prove to the officials that this is true."

I felt an anger burn inside me. I remembered how ugly the Haitian soldiers acted. Hadn't they killed Nicolas's father? And wouldn't they have killed Papi had they found him?

"I will go to the hearing," I promised. "I will tell them exactly what will happen if we go back to Haiti."

9

PAPI'S PLEA

December 5, 1991

We're still here! We had a little taste of Thanksgiving. Manmi was back with us to share it.

The cooks at the camp made turkey and pie. It was very good! Of course, Manmi said it would have been better with some of her roasted sweet potatoes.

Because there are so many of us in the camp, the hearings are taking forever. It is finally our turn tomorrow.

Ensign Jones has been helping me.

"Don't be scared," he said. "Just answer the questions as best you can."

"I wish you could be there," I said.

He smiled. "Just pretend I'm right beside you. I'll be thinking of you."

Now I can't sleep. Somewhere in the camp a baby is crying. I try to imagine what living in Miami will be like. But I can only think about tomorrow.

December 6, 1991

I felt like my legs were made of wood when we walked into the hearing room today. It reminded me of the principal's office in my old school in Haiti.

Four people sat at a long table. The two women wore Navy uniforms. Two others were immigration officials.

A thin lady at the end of the table was an **interpreter**. She told us in Creole that she would listen to our answers. Then she would tell them to the officials in English.

But Papi answered all of his questions in English. I could tell when his voice got loud that he was trying to make the officers understand how bad it was in Haiti. He talked for a long time. Once he waved his arms and shook his fist in the air.

Finally, Papi sat down. He wiped sweat from his face with a tissue. He smiled at me and patted my shoulder.

When my turn came, my tongue and mouth went dry. An immigration official said something to the interpreter.

"Tell us what you did in Haiti to help elect Mr. Aristide," she said.

I took a deep breath. That was easy!

"I handed out papers asking people to vote for him," I said. "Papi and I went to many villages and talked to people. I think we convinced many to vote for him. And he won!"

The lady nodded. She told the officials in English what I had said. One man nodded and smiled at me.

Then they asked me about the soldiers. I told them about the day they overthrew President Aristide. I told them about the soldiers killing people. I told them how they came almost every day looking for Papi.

I tried not to cry, but a tear rolled down my face. I swatted it away.

"We will all be killed if we go back," I finished.

Papi and I waited outside for the officials to make a decision. When they called us back in, the head official talked in English to Papi. A slow smile spread over Papi's face. The man handed him some papers and shook Papi's hand.

As Papi walked back to me, he didn't have to say anything. I knew we were going to America!

We celebrated tonight. Ensign Jones and his friends brought us popcorn and Cokes. They brought us some sweaters and jackets to take to Miami.

I feel happier than I ever remember feeling. But deep inside sits one sad thought. I will have to say good-bye to Ensign Jones.

10

FREEDOM!

December 14, 1991

I am writing this sitting on the white sand in Miami. We came here by boat from Cuba two days ago. My aunt and uncle met us at the dock.

"Welcome!" cried Tant Gisele.

Tears ran down her face. Papi is her older brother. She hugged him like she never wanted to let go.

Monnonk Claude gave Michele, Nicolas, and me little American flags. Then they took us to their home. Michele, Nicolas, and I will share one room.

After lunch, Monnonk Claude introduced us to their neighbors. Many Haitian families live around them.

The very next day, Tant Gisele took us to school. For the rest of this year, we will learn English there.

When we came home, Papi had good news. One of our new neighbors helped him find a job! He will be driving a taxi.

"I must get to know the city quickly," he said.

Yesterday afternoon, Papi and Monnonk Claude went out with maps. Papi must learn where places are so he can drive people to the right address. He is very proud of his bright yellow taxi.

Michele made friends right away with the girl next door. Nicolas made friends with her brother. They went off to a nearby park to play. But I am not ready to make friends yet.

Last night, Tant Gisele took Manmi, Nicolas, Michele, and me to see a movie. Such a big screen! I liked the music. But I could not understand the words.

Today is Saturday. Back in Haiti, I would be helping Manmi at the outdoor market. But here, we drove to a big indoor market. So many people! So much food! I miss the fun of our outdoor market. I miss the good smells. I miss the loud talking. Most of all, I miss meeting with our friends.

Right now, I also miss Ensign Jones. He gave me his harmonica when I left. I promised him that I would learn to play it.

I will end this now and try to play

a few tunes. But my heart will not be in it. My heart is back in Haiti.

December 24, 1991

Tomorrow is Christmas. All the houses here are covered with tiny lights. Tant Gisele and Monnonk Claude put up a tree in the living room. It is plastic.

Michele and Nicolas are all excited. Tant Gisele gave them money to buy presents for their new friends.

My Christmas present for everyone is that I learned to play some Christmas music on the harmonica. I will surprise them tomorrow.

I have learned many words in English. I met a girl at school who is helping me. Her name is Ana. She is 13 too.

Sometimes I still feel sad when I think of home. But I do love the freedom here. I am not scared to walk down the street. I am not scared that someone will hurt Papi.

We are having a big dinner tonight. Tant Gisele's house is full of people and good smells.

I slipped down to the beach to write this. I love my new family here. But just being alone sometimes helps me remember the people I left behind. Are they having a merry Christmas?

11

HAPPY NEW YEAR!

January 1, 1992
Happy New Year to me! I woke up
feeling special this morning—like
everything good is going to happen.

Last night, our neighborhood held a huge party. It ended with fireworks of every size and color.

"I love this!" Michele shouted, covering her ears. "Don't you?"

I nodded. The people around us were so kind! Last week, people from one church brought us boxes of clothes. They brought us pots and pans and towels too.

Over our school vacation, I read two books in English! Monnonk Claude and Tant Gisele gave them to me for Christmas.

"I have an announcement to make," Papi said this morning at breakfast. "In two days, we are moving to our very own apartment!"

"Yeah!" Michele cheered. "Can I have my own room?"

Papi patted her hair. "There is a little room that will be just for you. Nicolas and Louis will share a room."

Nicolas and I smiled at each other. Finally, we will have a room without nosy

Michele. There are no secrets with her around!

Tant Gisele asked me today if I had made a New Year's **resolution**.

"What's that?" I asked.

"It is something we do each New Year," she said. "We make promises to ourselves to change something or to try to do something better."

So I took my notebook down to the beach. It is where I think the best.

I thought all afternoon about what my resolution should be. I know that I want to be the best American I can be. I know I want to speak English well. I know that I want to be smart in school.

All these things would make good resolutions. But I think back to the promise I made to myself when I left Haiti.

Someday, I really do want to go back. I want to make things better for the people I left there. I don't know how I will do that.

Maybe if I study hard, I can go back as a doctor!

I look across the water. I cannot see Haiti. But I know it is there, just waiting for me.

"My New Year's resolution is that I will be back someday," I whisper to the ocean.

I know its waves will carry my message to Haiti.

AFTERWORD

Some refugees, like Louis, did return to Haiti.

In 1994, the United Nations and other countries helped the Haitian people. Together they made General Cedras promise to let President Aristide come back and rule Haiti.

President Clinton ordered 30,000 American troops to go to Haiti. Their job was to make sure the transfer of power from Cedras back to Aristide was peaceful.

On October 15, 1994, President Aristide returned in triumph to Haiti. People danced and celebrated in the streets.

Aristide served as president until December 1995. Rene Preval was elected to succeed him as president.

There are still problems between the military and the citizens of Haiti. But things are better for them now than they were in 1991.

The people of Haiti are strong and courageous. They will continue to fight to keep their freedom.

GLOSSARY

alternative   outside what's normal or expected

capsized   having been turned upside down

Creole   one of two languages spoken in Haiti. The other language is French.

dictator   person who rules a country without sharing power with anyone else

ensign   officer in the Navy with the lowest rank

granme   Creole word meaning "grandmother"

hounfor   Creole word for the place used for voodoo ceremonies

immigrant   person who comes to live in a country in which he or she was not born

independence   freedom from the control of others

interpreter   person who changes the words of one language into another language

Lavalas	President Aristide's political party
mambo	female voodoo priest. Voodoo is a religion practiced by many people in Haiti.
manmi	Creole word meaning "mother"
millennium	1,000 years
monnonk	Creole word meaning "uncle"
orphan	child whose parents are dead
papi	Creole word meaning "father"

refugee person who flees his or her country to find safety and protection elsewhere

resolution formal expression of intent; promise

rickety having an unsound physical condition

stern the back of a boat or ship

tant Creole word meaning "aunt"

tuberculosis disease that mainly affects people's lungs

vaccine   wooden flute
played by people in
Haiti

About the Author

Kathleen M. Muldoon is a staff writer for a local newspaper in San Antonio, Texas. In her free time, she likes to write for children. She is the author of a picture book, *Princess Pooh*, and her work has appeared in many children's magazines. She especially enjoys writing fiction and nonfiction involving animals and also loves to write original and retold folktales.

When not writing, Kathleen enjoys reading, visiting the many historical sites in Texas, collecting old postcards, and playing with her cat, Prissy.